Tales From East Anglia

Edited By Daisy Job

First published in Great Britain in 2018 by:

Young Writers
Remus House
Coltsfoot Drive
Peterborough
PE2 9BF
Telephone: 01733 890066
Website: www.youngwriters.co.uk

Book Design by Ashley Janson
© Copyright Contributors 2018
SB ISBN 978-1-78896-318-3
Printed and bound in the UK by BookPrintingUK
Website: www.bookprintinguk.com
YB0354L

FOREWORD

Young Writers was created in 1991 with the express purpose of promoting and encouraging creative writing. Each competition we create is tailored to the relevant age group, hopefully giving each child the inspiration and incentive to create their own piece of work, whether it's a poem or a short story. We truly believe that seeing their work in print gives pupils a sense of achievement and pride in their work and themselves.

Every day children bring their toys to life, creating fantastic worlds and exciting adventures, using nothing more than the power of their imagination. What better subject then for primary school pupils to write about, capturing these ideas in a mini saga – a story of just 100 words. With so few words to work with, these young writers have really had to consider their words carefully, honing their writing skills so that every word counts towards creating a complete story.

Within these pages you will find stories about toys coming to life when we're not looking, the adventures they have with their owners and even a few tales of peril when toys go missing or get lost! Each one showcases the creativity and talent of these budding new writers as they learn the skills of writing, and we hope you are as entertained by them as we are.

CONTENTS

Nayland Primary School, Nayland

Fionn Doyle (9)	54
Phoebe Atwill (9)	55
Lewis Crawford (9)	56
Rebecca Reason (9)	57
Harry Crisell (9)	58

Ravenswood Community Primary School, Ipswich

Debora Ida Harrris (10)	59
Sophie Pemberton (10)	60
Alanya-Lily May Evans (9)	61
Adele May (8)	62
Paige Willow Aust (11)	63
Celine Neal (11)	64
Patricia Stalnionis (9)	65
Winter Ivy Collins (9)	66
James Wood (10)	67

Sidestrand Hall School, Sidestrand

Billy Horler-Seaton (10)	68
Amy Davies (10)	69
Kane Bloomfield (10)	70
D'Arcy Broad (11)	71
Callum Stocks (11)	72
Ethan Starling (11)	73
Skye Williams (10)	74
Callum Baldwin (11)	75
Kieran Bennet (11)	76
Callum James Green (10)	77

St Augustine's Catholic Primary School, Old Costessey

Dave Joseph (7)	78
Jude David Ballentine (8)	79
Emilia Postle (7)	80
Erin McGhee (8)	81
George Dunscombe (8)	82
Takudzwa Satande (8)	83
Nikodem Przychodzko (7)	84

Jon Jacob Ereneta (7)	85
Noah Crew (7)	86
Henry George Cooknell (8)	87
Oliver William Herring (8)	88
Anabella Gracia-Climie (7)	89
Niamh Hogarty (8)	90
Harvey Bijosh (7)	91
Finlay Templeton (8)	92
Maria Pais Oliveira (8)	93
Elizabeth Anne Mitchell (7)	94
Ava Antonia Baxter (7)	95
Gabi Maria Moszczenska (8)	96
Emilia Sojka (7)	97
Darci-Ella Knott (7)	98
Pemisin Akinsiku (7)	99
Andre Dimaandal (7)	100
Angela Gabriella Thomas (7)	101
Kate Garchitorena (8)	102
Ben Schiller (7)	103
Jhenzel Daleon (8)	104
Andre Alphons (8)	105
Howard James Burke (7)	106

St Mary's Roman Catholic Primary School, Lowestoft

Olivia Marie Archer (9)	107
Samuel Amias Buhr (8)	108
Thomas Sewell (7)	109
Naomi Eleanor Sibbons (9)	110
Brooke LJ Matthews (8)	111
Thea Jackson-Tennant (9)	112
Mya Mckenna Reay-Smith (8)	113
Chaeli Knights (10)	114
Holly Burrows (7)	115
Gabrielle Elizabeth Lock (10)	116
Elijah Huke-Jenner (9)	117
Kailan Ansley (9)	118

Tattingstone CE (VC) Primary School, Tattingstone

Isobel Bond (8)	119
George Seager (10)	120
Layton Palmer (10)	121
Mia Joseph (9)	122
Holly Abbott (9)	123
Samuel Cocksedge (9)	124
Lily Mae Ransome (11)	125
Francesca Goodwin (9)	126
Alana Goodwin (8)	127
Isabel Knights (10)	128
Olive Potter-Cobbold (9)	129
Molly Wheatley (11)	130
Lilly Mai King (10)	131
Corban Zak Louka (9)	132

Walpole Cross Keys Primary School, King's Lynn

Isabella Hackett Morillo (11)	133

Wells-Next-The-Sea Primary And Nursery, Wells-Next-The-Sea

Milly Nudds (7)	134
Lily Wines (7)	135
Frances Emmerton (7)	136
Hollie Ellen Lovick (7)	137
Evie Moore (7)	138
Alfie Yaxley-Beckham (8)	139
Toby Wright (7)	140
Zachary Long (7)	141
George Wright (8)	142
Robert Smith (7)	143
Lily-Grace Jones (7)	144
Marley Daniels (8)	145
Ann-Marie Needham (7)	146
Cody-Liam Wyatt Lacey (7)	147
Freddie William Bix (7)	148

THE MINI SAGAS

Video Game Vs Toys

One day, when I was going along with my everyday life, I went out to school but what I didn't know was that my toys and video games came to life...

"Hey!" shouted Steve from Minecraft.

"Now what are you up to?" sighed Barbie.

"None of your business!" exclaimed Steve.

"This is war!" shouted Barbie.

"Stop!" exclaimed Marina as she magically came out from the Minecraft game.

"No one's ever done that before!" murmured Barbie.

"I'll tell you how I did that tomorrow. Oh no, she's coming, hide!" exclaimed Marina.

So they always got along.

Nicole Glover (8)
Admirals Academy, Thetford

When Toys Come Alive

Once upon a time, there was a twelve-year-old child who stole everyone's toys. When he got them he pulled them apart and made weird creations, and never put them back together properly or gave them back to their rightful owners. Unfortunately for him, the toys were alive and one night they decided to scare him, so that he would put them back together and give them back to their old owners. So that's what they did. He carefully put them back together with superglue and shone them up with polish and gave them back.

Laurence Roberts (10)
Admirals Academy, Thetford

The Christmas Reindeer

Ruby the reindeer was walking about in the forest, finding food. There were other animals around. The snow was on the ground as it was December and nearly Christmas. Ruby heard a noise and another reindeer appeared, his name was Jack. Jack was lost from his owner. The reindeer could hear someone calling, yes it was Jack's owner, Santa. Jack and Ruby called back in their own way so Santa knew where to find them. They could hear Santa getting closer and closer. Santa found Jack and his new friend, Ruby, and took them away to deliver the toys.

Fergus Steward (10)

Admirals Academy, Thetford

Texta Gets Into Trouble

When Mum and I went out, my toy dog, Texta, liked to play on the kitchen shelves. One day, he jumped on the shelves because he wanted to reach his ball. But he got so excited while he was throwing the ball around, he knocked over a whole tin of chocolate biscuits. It rolled down with a *thud, thud!* When Mum and I came home, we got a big surprise, there were chocolate biscuits everywhere. Mum was so angry she roared. She gave Texta away to the girl next door. She loved and cherished him. They lived happily ever after.

Emilia Grace Magnani (10)
Admirals Academy, Thetford

The Betrayer

One day, a girl called Jessie played with her doll in her bedroom. In the afternoon, Jessie went shopping with her mum and her doll, as they were inseparable. Suddenly, Jessie saw the world's fluffiest toy and she had to have it.

At night, Jessie slept with her new toy and left her doll on the bedroom floor. The next day, Jessie's neighbour came to play with her and saw the beautiful, lonely doll on the floor. Eagerly she asked, "Can I have it please?"

Jessie replied, "Of course, she's all yours!"

Mariana Costa Santos (9)

Admirals Academy, Thetford

Tom's Missing Gift

Santa was a very busy man. He was rushing to get away on time. Tom had been desperate for a cuddly panda all year. Once Santa was in the air, he realised he had forgotten Tom's toy. Searching through the sack, he managed to find an extra panda, except it had a missing eye. Santa had no time to find a replacement so he had to deliver it. Christmas morning, Tom excitedly unwrapped his presents, there was the panda but something was different about it. Looking closely, Tom noticed the missing eye but was overjoyed to have gotten his wish.

Sophie Kim Clarke (10)
Admirals Academy, Thetford

The Bear Came To Life

On a cold winter's morning, the air flew past Joe's face, he smiled and walked into the car to get ready to go to Butlins for a holiday. Joe was in for a surprise, his favourite teddy was shortly going to come alive, but Joe had no clue what this day's secret was holding.

When Joe left and slammed the front door behind him, his teddy, Buttons, woke up from the dead. He messed Tom's and his mum's room up. He only had time to mess around with one thing because Tom was coming back very soon.

Sophie Bishop (10)
Admirals Academy, Thetford

Mr McSnuffles

As I woke up, I soon realised I was sat on the cold, hard floor of the toy room. It was a bit odd because I knew that I went to sleep in my cosy bed with the squishy mattress. While I looked down to see if I was still in my pyjamas, I was shocked to see chestnut-brown, furry legs. Curiously, I felt all over my body to figure out if I was all fluff. To my surprise, I was sporting a humongous, tomato-red bow on my front. "Argh!" I had transformed into Mr McSnuffles!

Polly Lumley (10)
Admirals Academy, Thetford

Twister Competition

Woody and Buzz were doing a competition and were fighting over who was the best at Twister. They have been fighting since their owner, Eleanor, left the room for tea.

"I'm better!" Buzz murmured.

"No you're not, I am!" said Woody.

Jessie came in and whispered, "I'm better!"

"No you're not!" chanted Woody and Buzz together.

"Oh really," asked Jessie. "Let's have a game."

They played for ages. Woody murmured, "This is it, who's going to win?"

Bang! Buzz fell to the ground. Woody not far behind. Suddenly, Eleanor came running upstairs. Buzz, Woody and Jessie tidied up extremely fast.

Eleanor Moore (10)
Cedars Park Primary School, Stowmarket

The Moving Doll

"He, he, he! Everyone's asleep, that means I can do something a little bit naughty!" Lilly's doll, Penelope, is really naughty, she wakes every night and does disrespectful things.

Tonight, in her house, when everyone was asleep, Penelope trotted into the bathroom and lay in the bathtub.

"The sun is shining, what a beautiful day! I'm going to play with Penelope. Oh where is she? Oh well, I'll find her soon, I need to brush my teeth."

Lilly walked into the bathroom. "Argh!" Lilly screamed. She saw the doll. "Mum!" shouted Lilly to her mum...

Megan Fynn (10)
Cedars Park Primary School, Stowmarket

Santa's Other Little Helpers

It was Christmas night and Santa was in the house. After a long night, he spoke out to himself, "I'm too exhausted to do this, but who will if I don't?"

"I will!" objected Squidge, the cuddly penguin. With that, Squidge ran outside and grabbed Santa's sack of presents. He ran out onto the street and started to climb onto the roof of a house. He jumped straight down the chimney. Squidge walked around, making no sound and encountered nobody but a little kitten. He continued all through the night and when he was finished he became a real penguin!

Ben Atkins (9)

Cedars Park Primary School, Stowmarket

The Toys Fight

My name is Piggles, I'm a toy. My story starts when I got bashed. It was the night and it's my favourite time because I'm on my own with Half Horse. He is a Barbie but boy form. I started wandering about and I woke up Half Horse.

It was the next night and Hannah was having a sleepover with Romley and her boyfriend, George. "Right!" Half Horse shouted.

He decided to have a battle. That morning, under the bed they fought. They went on the window ledge. Half Horse fell down. He was finished. "Argh!"

"Bye-bye!"

Imogen Cook (8)

Cedars Park Primary School, Stowmarket

The Ballerina's Friends

There once were some ballerinas, they were awake every night playing silly games. One night, when they were playing a game, Emily saw them. The next day, Emily told her mum.

She said, "Tonight I will come and see," so she did and they didn't see anything because the ballerinas didn't move.

The next day, Emily's mum said, "How about you make friends with them?"

So from that day on, Emily and all the ballerinas played every day. They always were best friends but the ballerinas never showed up to any of the parents.

Nicole Tye (7)

Cedars Park Primary School, Stowmarket

The Toy

Ruby was playing with her doll and building blocks. The next morning, they were gone. She checked the toy box, her sister and her room but they weren't there. Then she asked her mum but she didn't know. Next, she asked her sister and found her looking guilty.

For nights and nights Ruby felt worried, she wanted to find out why her sister was guilty, so she got up from her bed and looked in her sister's wardrobe. There they were! Her favourite doll and building blocks. Her sister had taken them all along! But at least she's happy now!

Lauren Chapman (9)
Cedars Park Primary School, Stowmarket

Plastic Love

The princess sat next to her father.

"You must go to the toy tribute tumbler. There you will meet quite a dashing soldier," he said.

So the princess set off to the third tog tribute tumbler. As she reached her new destination, she saw the most handsome soldier in all of the omniverse. She grabbed him by the hand and said what was true to her heart.

"Dude, soldier of the north, I love you with all of my heart!" and with that he was thrust into her hands and as their lips touched, the air was filled with romance.

Duke Ecclestone (10)

Cedars Park Primary School, Stowmarket

Unfortunate Dolls

This was their chance. Elisiah and Jai (who were two dolls) were ready to escape. They climbed out the pale window, when *woof! Bark!* A rabid, ugly dog jumped into the room. With haste, they dived down. They found a cracked rock where they stayed for a few days. Soon, a small child found them and took them home. This child treated them with love and care. But that didn't last long. Years of joy passed. The child soon grew up and they were thrown in the bin. Did they survive and get out? No. Was it the end? No!

Isabella North-Fields (9)
Cedars Park Primary School, Stowmarket

Toy Happiness

There was a toy called Alice, she was stuck in a package and she longed for freedom, but she was locked in a case because she was the prettiest doll in the country. All of her friends had been taken away and sold to girls or mums for great birthdays or merry Christmases. Alice was getting very worried because she was not getting picked from the shelf and sold. She started to wonder if she was in a dream, but she kept telling herself that she wasn't in one.

"Wow!" exclaimed Alice with a jolting jump...

Isabelle Linney (9)
Cedars Park Primary School, Stowmarket

The Ripped Toy

One day, a girl called Casey went to a shop and got a cuddly lion toy and played with it every single day. She was the happiest girl. She ate marshmallows and drank hot chocolate and played with her toy.
The first night, the toy got ripped. When Casey woke up she cried because her toy had ripped, and demanded her mum get her a new one. She got a new one and loved it and it didn't rip.
"Yes!" she replied.

Casey Wilson (7)
Cedars Park Primary School, Stowmarket

Will Ant And Dec Get Out Of Here?

Suddenly, the Ant and Dec toys woke up.

"Where are we?" asked Ant.

"I don't know," answered Dec.

"It's pitch-black, what should we do?"

"Umm, let's feel around."

"OK," replied Ant.

"What's this stuff? It's all slimy," shouted Dec.

"I don't know," said Ant.

"Ouch!" screamed Dec. "Something bit me, maybe they're cockroaches or maybe it's little Dennis Wise."

"Of course he would be alone and lost as he's so small!" hollered Ant.

Dec shook his head in disbelief.

"What was that? I felt a big tail!" shouted Ant.

"Argh!" screamed both of them, yelling. "Get us out of hhhhhheeere!"

Sophia Luck (11)
Colneis Junior School, Felixstowe

The Mysterious Two Princesses

One day, in the great royal hall in the royal kingdom, there lived a magical princess. This magical princess had a hall with a bedroom that led to her magical hall, which only magical people could walk on. If you weren't magical, you could not walk on it.
One day, a girl dressed like a princess said, "Hello."
"I'm the magical princess here."
"Why were you in my room?"
"Mum!"
"Hello, who are you?"
"I'm Dorothy. My name's D.O.R.O.T.H.Y, the princess."
"So why can't there be two princesses?"
"That's a brilliant idea!"
"Quick, before the humans see!"

Skye Nico Furzer (8)
Colneis Junior School, Felixstowe

Amealia And The Panda Corn

Once, there lived a little girl called Amealia. One day, Amealia went out to town. Amealia walked past a toyshop called Toys And Me. It was the first time Amealia had been. In the window she saw a pandacorn.

Amealia couldn't keep the words in her mouth so she said, "Please, please can I buy that pandacorn?"

"No," said Mum.

"Why?"

"Because we need to save up for Florida next year," said Dad.

"How much is it?" said Mum.

"£100!"

"As we have got the money for Florida, we will buy her it."

"Yes."

"Thank you, Mummy!"

Olivia Turpin (8)
Colneis Junior School, Felixstowe

The Christmas Sergeant

"Morning guys," said Tommy.

"Morning," said Sergeant Pierson. "Soldiers out!"

"Pierson, I have a question for you," said Tommy.

"What is it, Boss?" said Pierson.

"I need you to infiltrate the dining room and find out my Christmas presents!" exclaimed Tommy.

"OK," Pierson said in a childish voice.

So Pierson and his five best men parachuted down from the top of the stairs to the dining room. They looked in the cupboard and they saw everything! So they went back upstairs and told Tommy about it all. But Tommy's mum had spotted the soldiers and swapped all the presents...

Ethan Bone (9)

Colneis Junior School, Felixstowe

The Imperfect Story

"He, he," laughed the Barbie doll. You may be wondering why the Barbie doll is laughing, well she is laughing at me. I'm Creepy Hand and I live in Toys 'R' Us, I have for about twelve years.

"You are so weird and creepy, Creepy Hand!" the wooden train cackled. "You're different from the other toys. No one will ever want you! You've been here for, what? Twelve years!"

"Yeah," I sighed.

Wait, someone is calling.

"I see a Creepy Hand. Can I get it? Please Mummy, please!"

Someone wants me! Well can't keep them waiting, can I? I'm wanted!

Ferne Hope (11)

Colneis Junior School, Felixstowe

Santa's Little Snow Friend

Last Christmas Eve, before Santa flew his sleigh, there was a mix-up between Rudolf and Bambi, a little girl's teddy. Ivy loved Christmas as much as she loved Bambi. Back at the North Pole, Bambi appeared.
"Who are you?" whispered Santa.
"I'm Bambi," Bambi cried. "Santa, can I help you?"
"Sure, with your bright colours you can lead the way!" said Donner.
So they flew up into the night. Suddenly, there was a flash of light. They were back at Santa's grotto.
"There you are, Bambi," cried Ivy, "let's play, where were you?"

Georgina Golding (8)
Colneis Junior School, Felixstowe

Elephanto

It's Monday and I'm off school with a cold. About an hour ago, I had a drink of water and accidentally spilt it on Elephanto, my teddy. And basically he came alive and jumped out of the open window. I screamed! Mum came rushing up the stairs.

"What's wrong?" she asked.

"Elephanto's gone!" I cried.

"Well let's find him!" she said confidently.

We ran out of the house and straight to the park. I searched and saw him sitting happily on a swing. He winked at me and I realised this was just the start of our epic adventures together.

Aoife Frances Moran (10)
Colneis Junior School, Felixstowe

Buddy To The Rescue

Bang! In the dim light of Jake's bedroom, Buddy, Jake's toy rabbit, had been startled by the sight of Santa, face down on the floor, motionless. Buddy knew he had to save Santa. He started his journey by dancing through twist and turn, then snakes and ladders, climbing up the stairs and sliding down the snakes. Next, onto Operation, making sure not to touch any of those edges! Finally, Buddy had to explore Mousetrap, being careful to not get caught. Buddy had saved Christmas with courage. Santa put the presents down for Jake, smiled at Buddy and disappeared with speed.

Saffron Luck (11)
Colneis Junior School, Felixstowe

Stinky The Slinky, The Unwanted Toy

Stinky the slinky was Amelia's favourite toy, until one day he was left behind and forgotten. Scared and worried, Stinky didn't know what to do. Left at the top of the staircase, does he jump to meet all of the other toys or does he stay alone? One day, whilst Stinky was staring down the staircase, he felt a tap on his shoulder.

"Hello," said a small bouncy ball. "My name's Bobby."

Bobby the bouncy ball had also been forgotten. There was a long silence, they looked at each other and with a glance at the staircase, off they went...

Riley Marie Britchfield (10)

Colneis Junior School, Felixstowe

This Is The Life Of The Toy Parrot

Once upon a time, an amazing toy parrot had some beautiful babies. When they grew up she told them, "It's time, you must find your own owners." The baby parrots found an owner in a flash, apart from the youngest, called Cuddles. She set off for an adventure to find a new owner.
He met some friends in the enchanted forest; Bernard, Mousey and Tigger. They knew a little girl who lived in the next village and showed Cuddles the way. The little girl fell in love with Cuddles straight away and had a happy life, they lived happily together.

Lillia Hicks (7)
Colneis Junior School, Felixstowe

A Little Toy Can Go A Long Way

"I can see it," said Toby the Lego block.
"It's beautiful," replied the Thunderbird Two action figure.
All Toby ever wanted was to get out from under the bed, and he'd done it! They could see the toy box and they planned to get inside it! On the way, they went past some Hot Wheels cars and tracks. Toby was so excited. He had been under the bed all his life. Thunderbird Two had been under there for longer. The toy box was a glory for them. Finally, they arrived. All the toys were staring at them, looking and whispering.

Eve Hope (11)
Colneis Junior School, Felixstowe

The Lonely Pig

Another day done at the charity shop. Pig sighed sadly. Cute cats, fluffy puppies, dolls and teddies all off to new homes. When was it going to be her turn? Didn't anyone like pigs?

Morning came, the sun was shining but Pig was sad. Big Ted had gone, Barbie too. Pig was thinking about who would be on the shelf with her tomorrow. Suddenly, a voice from below screamed, "Pig!" The voice got louder. Gentle hands took Pig down and she found herself being cuddled tightly by a little girl who stroked her and said, "Let's go home, Pig!"

Jessie Emerald Kennedy (10)
Colneis Junior School, Felixstowe

One Toy Became A Hero

Once upon a time, there was an ugly alien toy, he was mighty and his name was Timber. He lived on cold Mars. Timber didn't like it because there was not that much crime to fight. Then Timber started to build an incredible space rocket so they could go to wonderful Earth.

Ten hours later... when Timber got to Earth, he thought differently so tried to be like a normal person. It didn't end well. Timber thought sticks were bones. He didn't know any one of his friends had snuck on, so Vanoss stole his talent so Timber couldn't fight.

Leon Stewart Gillett (7)
Colneis Junior School, Felixstowe

United Teddy

Once upon a time, there lived a magical king, United and his teddy. United was playing with his teddy on his throne and then he went to get his lunch. When United got back, he noticed that his teddy had gone! United's servants said he shouldn't just walk into the dangerous woods to find his teddy but United was brave and loved his teddy. So United set off to the woods. United looked and looked and then he bumped into a fierce, fire-breathing dragon.
He said, "Come to my cave."
United went back home and Teddy was under his throne!

Imogen Hawtin (8)

Colneis Junior School, Felixstowe

The Adventures Of Gizmo The Pilot On His Supernatural Journey

Where am I? the pilot doll thought to himself, *I need to get out.* There was no escape. The pilot was lonely. He tried to call for help but nobody answered. Then he realised there was a hole where the drain is. The pilot climbed through the hole just to find himself in what looked like an alien spaceship. "Where are you going?" Alien asked. The pilot ran as fast as he could. Then another alien came along, he was trapped. The pilot didn't know what to do, the pilot ran but nobody knows what happened to the pilot.

Sienna Beales (11)
Colneis Junior School, Felixstowe

Jingly Goes To Center Parcs

Ethan gets Jingly the toy elf and takes him to Center Parcs. Jingly gets in the bath and has a shower. At midnight, Jingly goes in the sink with champagne and cucumber on his eyes.
Today, we go to a food place with an area to play in. A man said I pushed his baby. It made me sad. Tonight, we're going to roast marshmallows on the warm fire with Edie, Ethan, Jingly, Mum, Ivy, Darcy. Then sleep. Tomorrow we're going home but we can't forget what Jingly did. He sang 'Happy Birthday' to Ivy. Now we're all going home.

Ethan Phillips (7)
Colneis Junior School, Felixstowe

Bob Beats Guner!

Once upon a time, there lived a robot called Bob. Bob lived in a nice house that had nice flowers, comfy beds and a great TV. One day, when Bob came home from work he had been robbed! He was furious! The robber was his arch-enemy, Guner. Bob challenged Guner to a Nerf battle. The battle was raging. Guner had perfect shots in the middle of his back. Suddenly, Bob spun around and shot Guner in the middle of his chest. Bob had won the battle. Guner was a loser.
"Bye-bye," said Bob. "Don't mess with me again!"

Thomas Pilcher (7)
Colneis Junior School, Felixstowe

Santa's Snowy Friend

Once upon a time, there lived a girl called Kaitlyn and her friends, Kaylyn and Adela. It was Christmas Eve and everybody was putting their stockings up for Christmas Day. Me and my friends were so excited. I kept a box full of my Christmas toys.

In Santa's workshop, everybody was asleep ready for the night ahead, then one of the toys came alive. It was a white and black tiger! As Santa came to take the presents to the children, he kept the tiger as his snowy friend. They played hide-and-seek in the snow-covered trees.

Kaitlyn Marie Whiting (8)
Colneis Junior School, Felixstowe

Sam Saves The Day

One day in a house, lived a boy called Jack. For Christmas he had a toy, it was a teddy bear, he named it Sam. Then he had a horrible toy for his birthday, the toy's name was Cybetron, he tried to harm all the toys. Then Sam sprinted and defeated the toy by throwing everything he could see on him.

"Ha, ha, ha, I defeated the horrible Cybetron."

After that, Cybetron ran away. He said, "You haven't seen the last of me."

So Sam saved the day from horrible Cybetron.

Vaishnavi Ganesh (8)
Colneis Junior School, Felixstowe

The Robot Monster

Once upon a time, there was a toy called the Robot Monster. He lived in a deep, deep cave underground. Once, he dug up and up. One day he came into the real world, he saw these animals, he thought they were called dinosaurs. One dinosaur stomped on him. They were so heavy he couldn't get up. After he did get up, the day before Christmas, he rushed to get his slimy, sloppy decorations and Christmas tree. But that night he stayed up too late, Santa came down the rusty chimney and he had to go back up the chimney.

Finley James Saynor (7)
Colneis Junior School, Felixstowe

Jealous Teddy

It's Christmas in Dan's house and he loves his toys. But his favourite is Robot and Teddy was jealous. So he came up with a plan, a plan to steal all the presents to attract Dan's attention.

So on Christmas Eve, when the house was silent, he came out of his toy form and threw all the presents into the icy snow. Suddenly, the lights turned on upstairs. He hid back in Dan's room as fast as he could. He put Robot next to the tree so it looked like he did it. What happened next? Did Teddy get revenge?

Maisie Beardwood (11)

Colneis Junior School, Felixstowe

Lost And Found

Once, there was a girl called Penny. She had a special toy cat called Jinx who she loved a lot. Penny loved Jinx so much that she took him to see Santa when she delivered her list. When she got home, Jinx was missing. Penny looked everywhere but he could not be found. Christmas would not be the same without Jinx and even when Penny opened her presents, she was still sad. As she opened her last present, she was thrilled to see Jinx inside. He must have got lost with Santa and had finally made his way back home.

Darcey Duffield (8)
Colneis Junior School, Felixstowe

My Dream-Catching Alajacorn

I'm an Alajacorn, I'm a unicorn teddy crossed with a fairy and I was bought for my owner, Lauren. What she doesn't know is that whenever she has a bad dream, I'm the one who fights them away for her... She's having one now, I can tell because she's twitching in her sleep. This is where I come in. I fly down to her pillow and I touch my horn onto her head and then I'll throw it in the bin and that bad dream is gone forever! I just hope one day she realises I magic her dreams away!

Alexia Bell (11)
Colneis Junior School, Felixstowe

Windy Days

Hi, I'm Kevin the kite. I spend most of my time in a garden shed until it gets windy. Then I'm taken out and thrown up into the air on a long piece of string. I'm expected to perform somersaults and often I come down with a crash that leaves me with lots of bruises. As soon as the wind stops, I'm not needed any more and I'm stuck back in the shed until another windy day arrives. I really don't look forward to windy days, but my owners do. I just wish they knew how I felt sometimes.

Ellie-Rose Edwards (11)
Colneis Junior School, Felixstowe

A Genie In A Bottle!

There was a little girl who, for her birthday, got a genie lamp but little did she know inside were three wishes. She thought it was a toy or some kind of ornament.

A few days later, her friend came round, her name was Caity. She knew about the three wishes and wanted them for herself. So when she was about to leave the house, she snatched the lamp so no one could see. She ran out the door. When she got back, she rubbed the lamp and said, "Can I have a toy?" and out popped a genie...

Charlotte Albins (10)

Colneis Junior School, Felixstowe

Lost And Found

Once, there was a girl called Elsie. Her mum and dad went to the shops and Elsie was at home on her own; well, with Max. Max was her favourite toy. She played with him all day.

A couple of hours later, Elsie noticed that her mum and dad didn't come home. So she bought Max to life and went to go look for them. She went to the shops. They were going too but they weren't there, so she went back home, up to her room and her parents were there. They were a little emotional, but they hugged.

Scarlett Downes (9)
Colneis Junior School, Felixstowe

Ballerina

Once upon a time, there was a girl doll called Beauty the ballerina. She loved ballet, it was her favourite thing to do, but then she heard a freaky voice. She carried on doing ballet, but why was she a rude girl to everyone? She knew everyone thought she was kind when she found a new friend. She started getting kinder and kinder, then she really liked kind games. Now people think she is kind and they have lots of fun together, and that's how Beauty the ballerina became nice.

Orlina Idrizi (7)
Colneis Junior School, Felixstowe

The Magic Bed

On a magical bed, there was a pig called Jack and a witch called Wiz. They were a boy's cuddly toys. One day, the boy was out and his magic bed made a funny spell. The spell made the toys come alive. The wicked witch did not like Jack. So when Jack wasn't looking, the witch made a spell that turned Jack into a normal cuddly toy. When they got back, his mum said, "Clear up!"
The witch shouted, "Ha, ha!"
So the boy threw the witch into the bin. Back to normal!

Oliver Bloomfield (8)
Colneis Junior School, Felixstowe

Unicorn Cupcake

Cupcake lived in a special castle. It was made out of cake. But it was very strong because it was so special that it was made out of Cupcake's favourite colours. It was amazing because the best chef in the world made it. Cupcake was very excited to live in it. It was very colourful. It was amazing because it was a very pleasant place to live. It looked very pretty. It was so big. It was a very old building so one day it rotted away. They had to build a whole new one, it was very fresh.

Poppy Jane Wilkes (7)
Colneis Junior School, Felixstowe

A Christmas Day And Night Party

Once upon a time, there lived a boy. He was opening his Christmas presents and his mummy and daddy gave him a present. He opened it and it was a toy ghost and it lit up like a bright, glittering star. The boy got so excited, he danced around the house like a mouse going crazy. He got so excited, he was so delighted. He sent lots of invitations to everyone in the street and he had the biggest party ever, and he was dancing all night and they all lived happily all day.

Macy Jefferson (8)
Colneis Junior School, Felixstowe

Bank Spy

One night there was a toy pig. He was guarding the bank. It was 12am but he was so tired he fell asleep. A burglar cracked the window and stole the money. The pig woke up but he did not catch the thief. So the next night he pretended to fall asleep and the robber came in, but the pig called the police and he got caught and went to jail. He had to pay a big fine. It was about £6,500 but he escaped. He got caught again and had to pay the fine again.

Maisie Loretta Tonks (10)
Colneis Junior School, Felixstowe

The Night Of The Lego Man

A long time ago, there was a Lego man desperate to get some toys. Then that night, he thought of a plan. The plan was to break into a toy store so he could get some toys. Finally, it was the night to break into the store so when everyone was asleep, he went to the toy store and he bought a Lego crowbar to break into the toy store. So he got in and got loads of toys. The next day was Christmas and he got no toys.

Finn Westley (8)
Colneis Junior School, Felixstowe

Chewy And The Space Dinosaur

One regular day, Chewy went for a walk round the toy shelf, he found a dinosaur and a space boat. Chewy screamed in his head, *What? A dinosaur in a boat?* Chewy then jumped onto Dean the dinosaur's back. Chewy saw a big red button and slapped it silly. The big red button sent Chewy flying with the dinosaur in the air. They flew so fast they hit into a gigantic Stormtrooper's gun and crashed into a gigantic ship. The boat shot a missile at the ship and Stormtrooper. Chewy flew to the moon and had a party.

Jordan Macey (9)
Compass Pott Row, Pott Row

Tiger And Molly's Super Adventure

One day, Tiger and Molly were playing in my room. Then they found a magic key on the floor. It was glowing. Tiger said, "Oh it's a key glowing, let's bring it on top of the bed." Tiger picked it up in his mouth and it glowed rainbow colours, and in a flash turned him and Molly into real dogs. Then they jumped off the bed and the magic key disappeared, and there were lots of dogs like pugs outside the house. The magic key had turned all toy dogs into real dogs everywhere. I came back and was happy.

Blake Pain (10)

Compass Pott Row, Pott Row

Santa's Little Toy

Once upon a time, there lived a man called Santa Claus (you know him) and a cheeky toy elf called Happy. They shared a cottage and worked extremely hard, day and night. Happy had a special power of telling the future. Every year, Santa would ask, "Will I get mince pies?" Happy would always answer, "Yes."

However, something awful happened. The elf lost his ability to see into the future. This meant Santa had to read all the letters children had sent. He sighed and went to bed. The next morning, Happy returned to normal again. Never give up hope!

Trinity Grimsey (11)
Laureate Community Academy, Newmarket

Robber And His Money

Once, there was a toy monkey called Robber which came alive. Robber found a mysterious car... He climbed into the car, started the engine and then he sped off, in a flash. Suddenly, Robber found himself in prison. He didn't know what to do. But then he found something strange. Robber picked it up and then said a few words, then *boom!* The wall crashed to bits... Robber ran. Then Robber found a building with the word 'Bank' on. The next second, Robber was in the vault collecting all the money he could... The police arrived. Robber fell asleep!

Fionn Doyle (9)
Nayland Primary School, Nayland

The Teddy Bear And The Carousel Horse

The clock struck twelve. Everyone was asleep except me and my sister's teddy bear. We jumped out our window portal and landed in the theme park. Ted the teddy bear jumped onto the carousel horse, then something happened. The horse came to life and rode us into the clouds, but we didn't like it there because the cloud monkeys were fighting with cloud balls so we left. Then we went to the park and played in the castle but the knight was slaying the dragons. We tried to speak but they didn't reply so we went back home.

Phoebe Atwill (9)
Nayland Primary School, Nayland

The Hungry Horse

A horse was galloping to a gingerbread man's house. Then he saw a gingerbread man that was slowly walking on the path. He was going to a gingerbread man's house because he was hungry and he wanted to eat. Suddenly, he saw a gingerbread man and he thundered, "Hello."
Just then, he saw a human! He ate the gingerbread man that was very tasty and he galloped away. Although he thought he was alone, he noticed lots of horses. He ran with them but one of them hit him and he lost them. After that, he was just a toy.

Lewis Crawford (9)
Nayland Primary School, Nayland

The Time Machine!

One morning, Oliver was out in the garden with his favourite toy, Rex. At 12 o'clock, Oliver was downstairs eating his lunch. In his bedroom was a time machine, Rex strolled into it and went back in time. First, he met the Romans, had a battle against the Celts and won! Next, he went to Unicorn Land and flew to the moon. Suddenly, the unicorn shook its mane and sweets fell out. Then he jumped into a rocket and zoomed back home. Then, Rex jumped into the toy box, until Oliver came up to play with Rex again before dinner.

Rebecca Reason (9)

Nayland Primary School, Nayland

Cursed Lego

One day, a boy bought a box of Lego. It said 'Lord of the Rings: Golden Chamber'. He started building the people.

His mum yelled, "Bedtime!"

He turned the lights off and climbed into bed. *Bang!* The box fell. The Lego people climbed out. They went under the bed and they built the dragon and crept to the boy and tied up the boy. They burned the house and village down. Flame after flame after flame, they went to Smyths Toys Superstore and lived happily ever after.

Harry Crisell (9)
Nayland Primary School, Nayland

The Teddy Bear

Once upon a time, a teddy named Emily set out for an adventure to look for her friend, Ruby but she did not know what was ahead...

She woke up and screamed, "Somebody help me please!" That's when she heard footsteps... It was Ruby, she couldn't believe it.

"Why?" she asked.

"Well you see, I'm a little old for you young teddies, nobody wants an old teddy like me," replied Ruby.

"Come home with me, my owner will love you," said Emily.

"OK then," said Ruby.

Then she woke as it was a dream and Emily lived happily ever after.

Debora Ida Harrris (10)

Ravenswood Community Primary School, Ipswich

Possy Penguin And The Christmas

It was Christmas and Possy Penguin was very excited because she was going to meet Father Christmas. Possy packed her bags and walked to Santa's grotto. When she got there, she felt special and important until Possy Penguin slipped on a banana peel (that one of the elves dropped earlier).

"Argh!" shouted Possy as she slid down the hallway and oh no, she broke all of the machines. Now Christmas was ruined.

Santa came rushing in. "Oh no, my machines!" he said.

"Don't worry, Santa," said Possy. "We can fix it in time."

So Possy and Santa finished in time.

Sophie Pemberton (10)
Ravenswood Community Primary School, Ipswich

Daisy's Christmas Gift

Once upon a time in Winter Wonderland, there lived a pink-coloured unicorn called Daisy. She was in her house minding her own business. It was Christmas, she was so excited. She went out and found Storm. She asked if she could have a snowball fight with her but Storm said, "No, because no one likes you." Daisy ran home and when she entered, there sat Santa.
"Daisy, what would you like for Christmas?"
She replied, "Some friends," then he disappeared.
On Christmas morning, Daisy woke to find all the unicorns waiting to play snowball with her outside.

Alanya-Lily May Evans (9)
Ravenswood Community Primary School, Ipswich

Untitled

Ten years ago, there was a toy monkey called Micky, he had a wife called Minnie and here is their tale. Micky was born in 2008.
"Minnie, where is the car?"
"I put it in the garage."
One stressful night, Minnie woke up and noticed that Mickey was gone. She also noticed that he had turned savage. Mickey was in hospital at the time. Minnie was worrying. "Are you OK?" she wondered.
So you're probably wondering what they did when Mickey came out of hospital. Well, they had Christmas and got married and had children named Charli, Rosie and Finley.

Adele May (8)
Ravenswood Community Primary School, Ipswich

The Ghostly Trials Of A Toy Penguin

Pip hasn't had a family, he has always just roamed the streets. One day, something peculiar happened. Something that has no explanation. "Help!" Pip squealed, trying to scramble out of the tiny box.

Before he could scream, he was flying through the air, he'd fallen out of a plane! Once he was on the solid ground, Pip had to play tough games, defeat robots and a mean toy whale. After he'd tackled these toys, he finally reached a warm cosy igloo in which made him feel alive, he really had a family. Pip and his new friends all gathered around.

Paige Willow Aust (11)

Ravenswood Community Primary School, Ipswich

Barbie And Ken

Early Monday morning, Barbie woke up to a new school year. She was now in Year 8. In her maths class was a really cute boy called Ken. She didn't know if he liked her but she knew that she liked him. After lunch, Ken plucked up the courage to ask her to the 'back to school' disco. She replied, "Yes, definitely!"
On Friday (disco day), Barbie had gone out to buy a really nice dress. At the disco, he said that she looked amazing! After a few seconds, they finally kissed.
Ten years later, they are still together.

Celine Neal (11)
Ravenswood Community Primary School, Ipswich

The Enchanted Dragon

In an enchanted forest, on an enchanted mountain range, there lived a dragon, its name was Dazzle. Dazzle lived in the forest, but one day she heard the voice of Dippley Doll. "I see a big tree and above it, a dragon."
Dazzle heard her and swooped down deep into the forest to hide. While Dazzle was hiding, she looked at the sun and amount of light. She was saved because when it gets dark, all the living toys turn back to being frozen toys. As Dippley entered the forest, she only had ten seconds. They all became toys.

Patricia Stalnionis (9)
Ravenswood Community Primary School, Ipswich

The Reborn Doll

When Kate tidied her room, her mum gave her twenty pounds to buy a new Reborn doll. When Kate arrived at the shop, she saw many dolls. Kate could not decide which one she wanted. A few moments later, she found the doll she had been looking for. Kate bought her doll and went home. The next day, Kate noticed her doll had disappeared and there was only a box to be seen. Kate ran to her mum's room but wait, her mum was not here, instead her mum's room was filled with Reborn dolls, they were wrecking the room.

Winter Ivy Collins (9)
Ravenswood Community Primary School, Ipswich

The Toy That Made A Kid's Day

One day, a toy was brought to Toys 'R' Us. But he didn't get sold, he waited every day for someone to choose him. One day, the owner came along with lots of kids on a school trip. Many of them walked by but none noticed him. One day, a shy kid was at the back of the herd of younglings, he noticed the toy. He had some money to spend on toys and was allowed to pick a toy to take home. The kid ran to the toy and took it home, and they became friends for evermore.

James Wood (10)
Ravenswood Community Primary School, Ipswich

Evolution To Devolution

"Bye toys! See you soon," called Billy.

"Guys it's time, get out of the toy box! He's gone! Teddies get out of the pile, he's out! Come on Pikachu, let's start the fun!"

"OK!" said Pikachu.

Under the bed Pikachu found a mysterious, shiny stone. He touched it... "Guys, I feel weird..."

"Oh, he's evolved!"

"I don't like it! Change me back!"

"We can do that but there is a risk involved!"

The toys crept downstairs to find the devolution spray... "Here you go!"

"Wow, I'm better!"

"Quick Billy's back, let's hide!"

"Hi toys, hello! That's weird, you're over there..."

Billy Horler-Seaton (10)
Sidestrand Hall School, Sidestrand

Santa's Lost Hat

One Christmas Eve, Santa lost his hat. "I'm sad!" he said.

"Don't be sad!" said Rainbow. "I'll help you!"

Amy went to the park. She came back, went upstairs and opened the door. Rainbow shouted to Santa, "Quick, Amy's coming!"

Amy went into the bedroom. "Oh dear, I thought I put Santa on my bed but now he's in the toy box... Santa, where's your hat?"

Amy went downstairs and told Mum Santa was in the toy box. "I thought you left him on your bed?"

"I did!" said Amy.

"Never mind," said Mum, secretly she knew something Amy didn't...

Amy Davies (10)
Sidestrand Hall School, Sidestrand

Untitled

Pudsey Bear was helping Santa on Christmas Eve to deliver the presents to all of the children all over the whole world. Rudolph was pulling the sleigh through the night, looking good with his shiny red nose! It was snowing hard, the reindeer were dashing through the snow.
Suddenly, Santa shouted, "Stop! Wait here!"
The sleigh came to an abrupt stop. "There's something in the snow!" exclaimed Pudsey Bear. "It's a toy robot with a Christmas hat on!" Pudsey picked up the robot and put it in the sleigh. "I wonder how it got there?" The robot winked at Santa...

Kane Bloomfield (10)
Sidestrand Hall School, Sidestrand

The Mystery Of The Chocolate Ranger

It was night, it was dark. Red Ranger crept downstairs. He had to be careful nobody saw him, he didn't want to get caught! He aimed for the kitchen and cake! In he went, heading straight for the fridge. He opened the door, the light came on! "Oh no!" he whispered to himself.

He looked around, nobody had seen. Into the fridge he reached and took out a huge piece of chocolate cake! He took a massive bite! Back to D'Arcy's bedroom he went.

In the morning, D'Arcy found him, "Hmm... why is the Red Ranger's face covered in chocolate?"

D'Arcy Broad (11)
Sidestrand Hall School, Sidestrand

The Friendly Dinosaur

One day, Callum went out. Sergeant and his army went back to their army base in Callum's bedroom. They heard a noise, they stopped for a minute then they saw an enormous dinosaur. They were terrified. They ran for cover, shaking in their boots! Then the dinosaur said, "Hi guys, can I come with you to your army base?"

They went back and had a party, he was a friendly dinosaur.

Callum came home, he went upstairs to his bedroom. He saw his toy box was open. Dinosaur was in the army base.

"How did you get there?" asked Callum.

Callum Stocks (11)

Sidestrand Hall School, Sidestrand

The Army Man Who Left The Room

One day, Morgan was fast asleep. One of his army toys fell off the side. Suddenly, all of the toys in Morgan's room came alive. They had to be super quiet. All of the toys climbed up on each other's backs to open Mum's door for the army men. He pushed his way through. Suddenly, the door went *bang!* Mum woke up. All of the toys stood still, Mum stepped on the army man. "Ouch!" cried Mum. Mum walked to Morgan's room. "Morgan, why are your toys in my bedroom? Morgan, wake up!"

"I don't know, I was asleep, Mum!"

Ethan Starling (11)
Sidestrand Hall School, Sidestrand

The Naughty Baby Doll

Skye was asleep. Baby Annabell crept out of bed and went downstairs. It was dark. Annabell went into the lounge and woke Baby Bobby up! They went to the kitchen. Annabell got Coco Pops out of the cupboard.

Bobby said, "No Annabell! That's naughty!"

Annabell didn't listen, she tried to put the cereal in a bowl but she made a huge mess on the floor! She went to the fridge to get the milk, it was very heavy, she dropped it! The milk went on the floor! When Skye woke up, Mummy made her clear up the mess she'd made...

Skye Williams (10)
Sidestrand Hall School, Sidestrand

The Haunted Toy

Once, there was a boy called Callum. He got a teddy for Christmas but what Callum didn't know was that the teddy came alive, it was haunted! Teddy liked to change the house into different countries when nobody was around. But when someone found out, one of their favourite toys would disappear, never seen again!

One day, Callum came home from school, finding the house was in LA! He was worried! Callum went to his bedroom and found his favourite toy dog was gone. He was upset, he went to look for it but nobody knew he had gone...

Callum Baldwin (11)

Sidestrand Hall School, Sidestrand

Lost Teddies

Kieran went downstairs to have lunch. All the teddies and Bumblebee went to the sweet shop to get some sweets. On the way they went missing. Kieran wondered where they were. Someone had taken them! Kieran tried to find them, he looked everywhere. He called the police. The police went to find the toys. They found the person who had the teddies and returned them to Kieran. Kieran was so glad to have them back, especially as it was Christmas. He gave the police a mince pie! The toys were glad to be home. They had a big party.

Kieran Bennet (11)
Sidestrand Hall School, Sidestrand

The Lost Tractor

Ben lost his favourite tractor at the park. It was time to go home and Tractor was lost. The tractor started to move on its own. He was trying to get back to the bedroom but didn't know the way. He needed to find a sign to help him. He travelled over the hills. He found a sign with the name of where he needed to go, but it's a long way to travel and Tractor was tired. Luckily, along came a car. Tractor jumped and managed to climb on. The car drove straight past his house, he was home.

Callum James Green (10)
Sidestrand Hall School, Sidestrand

The Infinite Jungle

One Saturday night, Sonic and Tails were exploring the infinite jungle.

"How long do you think we've been out for? It looks pretty dark," said Tails.

"We'll be fine," replied Sonic.

Suddenly, they heard scuffling. They turned around and saw a massive hedgehog.

"Hi, I'm Barry," he said.

"Argh! Run!" exclaimed Tails.

They turned and ran but they didn't know which way to go.

"I'm going to eat you!" Barry said.

Then Daniel (their owner) stared down and he said, "There you are."

He picked them up and went inside. "I'll get you and I'll eat you both!" said Barry.

Dave Joseph (7)
St Augustine's Catholic Primary School, Old Costessey

The Big Bounce

"No! Shugs, we can't bounce like you, we're not rabbits!"

Shugs was sad that none of his friends could bounce with him. As he was looking out the window, he stopped.

"Guys, I've got a really good idea. Jude's trampoline!"

"OK," agreed the others and they all headed to the garden.

"Wow!" said Darth Vader.

"This is amazing!" said Rexy.

A car pulled into the driveway.

"Oh no!" exclaimed Shugs. "Jude's coming back. Follow me!" called Shugs, thinking quickly.

He bounces straight in Jude's open window, and the toys land on the bed just as Jude opens the door. Phew!

Jude David Ballentine (8)

St Augustine's Catholic Primary School, Old Costessey

The New Toy

"Look!" shouted Bonnie to Zac. "There's a new toy here. Let's go and see what her name is," and Bonnie ran over to it.

Zac said, "Why don't we stay here?"

Bonnie then called Zac a 'scaredy-cat'!

Bonnie reached for the new toy and said, "What is your name?"

The toy was very shy. The toy replied, "My name is Holly."

They then started playing together.

Then Zac said, "That's it, you two are getting split apart!"

They replied, "Noooo!"

Holly was then put into a cage.

"Ouch!" cried a big person called Danny, who was then walking by.

Emilia Postle (7)
St Augustine's Catholic Primary School, Old Costessey

The Lost Voice!

"Plu, plu, plu!" Squiggle splutters.
"He's lost his voice!"
This is bad because he's got a singing test today. His neighbour, Deena the dinosaur, hears his splutters, so she goes to have a look. She comes over and shouts, "Oh no, you have singing. You need some help. Lie down and have some hot honey. Now go to bed."
The next day Squiggle gets out of bed and sings, "Good morning!"
Deena says, "You sang!"
The judges look stern. Simon, a judge says, "Go on then."
So Squiggle does. Afterwards, he comes out and sings, "I passed!"
"Yay!" says Deena.

Erin McGhee (8)
St Augustine's Catholic Primary School, Old Costessey

Echidna's Long Lost Cousin

"Excuse me, have you seen my long-lost cousin?" cried Echidna.

"No," said Wombat, "what does he look like?" Echidna was sitting on the huge bed with his friend Wombat and they were chatting really loudly. Suddenly, the Beanie Boos came up to them and said excitedly, "We think that we found him." Slowly, a hedgehog came up to him but then he waddled off. After that, something weird happened. A very weird animal came up to them and Echidna said, "Who are you?"

"I'm Platypus, your cousin."

"But you've got a duckbill and flippers," said a confused Echidna.

George Dunscombe (8)
St Augustine's Catholic Primary School, Old Costessey

Amando's Shocking Secret

I came back home and removed my shoes, went upstairs, opened my wardrobe and then the next thing I saw was Amando partying with my other teddies. After that, there was silence for a few minutes and then I called, "Amando, do you really do this when nobody is at home?" I said this in a confused voice.

"Yes," said Amando, scared and worried.

"Wow!" I said surprisingly. "You can really talk and move," I said. "But why didn't you tell me?"

"It's because I was scared you might faint."

"Aww, it's alright Amando, but never keep a secret again!"

Takudzwa Satande (8)
St Augustine's Catholic Primary School, Old Costessey

The Picture

Once upon a time, Teddy Pig did a drawing but he didn't know what it was so he asked his mum and dad what it was. They didn't know either.

"It's time for bed, Teddy Pig," Mum said.

Teddy Pig went upstairs. He couldn't sleep because he was thinking about the drawing.

Next morning, Teddy Pig was tired. First thing in the morning he asked Bing Bong and Doughnut, "What's the drawing?"

They didn't know, now he went to the drawing place. The drawing place was five hours away. He's going now.

Five hours later, the drawing place knew.

"Pineapple?"

Nikodem Przychodzko (7)
St Augustine's Catholic Primary School, Old Costessey

Lego Warriors

Once, there were four Lego warriors trying to get out of the city because there were bombs around. "Alert. Do not go inside the building as there are some bombs," said the captain.
"The bomb is about to explode!" said Warrior Three.
"Hey, do you know where Warriors Eighty-Two, Eighty-Three and Eighty-Four are?" said Warrior Eighty-One.
"I think they're either killed, went inside the buildings or went somewhere else maybe," said Warrior Four.
"I think the time on that bomb is 8:60," said Warrior One. "Run, run, run! There's the end of the maze!"

Jon Jacob Ereneta (7)
St Augustine's Catholic Primary School, Old Costessey

![Young Writers logo]

The Lost Soldier

On Christmas Eve, the soldiers were marching, but one soldier was lost. Don't worry, there is a person with binoculars.

So the captain said, "Hey you, yes you, can we borrow your binoculars for a second?"

They couldn't see anyone but there was something big and shaped like a triangle.

"Wait," shouted one voice. "It's a Christmas tree, let's climb up it and it's so big we will be able to find the last soldier" and they did, but that moment a big 'ho, ho, ho' was heard.

"Quick!" said the captain. "Prepare for attack!"

Noah Crew (7)

St Augustine's Catholic Primary School, Old Costessey

The Lost Colonel

Colonel Cooknell was out on an expedition. "I must find those dangerous dinosaurs," he said.
The soft terrain of the sofa proved to be very difficult but he was sure that he could overcome any obstacle. Suddenly, he fell between two cushions. The Colonel was lost but wasn't going to give up hope. He looked around and found everything but dinosaurs. A KitKat, a 50p coin and even Sergeant Sandwich. Henry, their owner, then reached down and grabbed them. Henry was delighted! He had found soldiers, money and chocolate! The Colonel was safe but the dinosaurs would have to wait!

Henry George Cooknell (8)

St Augustine's Catholic Primary School, Old Costessey

The Day The Football Figures Went To Wembley

William bought eight football figures. The first was Cristiano Ronaldo. William had to leave for school. The football figures went outside and a portal appeared and took them to Wembley Stadium. There were lots of fans and they played a four-a-side football match. Ronaldo was sent off for a dangerous slide tackle. Paul Pogba scored an overhead kick, the crowd went wild. The portal reappeared and the players ran at top speed to get back in the portal. They arrived home and found William looking for them. Ronaldo hid a trophy behind his back to surprise William.

Oliver William Herring (8)
St Augustine's Catholic Primary School, Old Costessey

Hugo The Bear And His Secret Mission

I went to school. Hugo the bear and his friends quickly got out of bed and ran downstairs. My dad put special cameras on today. We think they're moving. They are because they're doing special meetings. They're doing it in a special place in the cupboard under the stairs. They open the doors and they've got cakes. The meeting is about a meteorite that's going to crash on Earth. So they gather up all the teddies from the world and they all make a ginormous trampoline.

The meteorite bounced. It flew away. They all cheered happily.

Anabella Gracia-Climie (7)
St Augustine's Catholic Primary School, Old Costessey

The Adventure Of Acrobat Niamh

The shop had closed for the day and Acrobat Niamh woke up from her nap. She stretched and said, "Time to practise some gymnastics." And off she went. She swung off the lights. She cartwheeled over the tiles and backflipped over aisles. Suddenly, the alarm went off. The police came and they saw a man walking by the shop, carrying a bag outside the shop and thought he set the alarm off. Niamh said, "This is my fault!" They let the man go and said to themselves, "I can't believe I've seen a talking doll."

Niamh Hogarty (8)
St Augustine's Catholic Primary School, Old Costessey

The Live Racing Car

There was a flash behind the sofa. It was a racing car. Its name was Lightning 1. He raced around the house. When he raced by the table, he met a gang. He thought he could join the gang but they said no.

The racing car asked, "What about a race?"

They said, "Yeah!"

So they went to a stadium outside the house where they could race each other. Then they got on the race track. They had ten laps on the track and the racing car won. Suddenly, they heard noises of a giant called Harvey B.

"Oh no..."

Harvey Bijosh (7)

St Augustine's Catholic Primary School, Old Costessey

The Creepiness Intensifies

Once upon a time, there were ten soldiers, they had to move outside otherwise they would die. They came from under the bed, through the door, down the stairs and around the kitchen where they found some tanks. They marched to the tanks, then they spotted some artillery. They grabbed the tanks and drove over to the artillery. They hooked the artillery onto the tanks and drove off heading towards their big escape.

Suddenly, a boy came running in and said, "What?" Then he tidied away the toys and sat down on a chair.

Finlay Templeton (8)

St Augustine's Catholic Primary School, Old Costessey

The Total Escape

Once upon a time, BoomBoom was planning to escape, she was on the floor. She got up and tried to escape through the bedroom window. It didn't go well so she tried the cupboard door because she thought it was the door which led to the living room, and it also didn't go well. She tried the last door. She ran into the door and really hurt her nose. The door suddenly opened and she saw a person. The person said, "What are you doing here? I put you away."
The person put the teddy away on the bed.

Maria Pais Oliveira (8)
St Augustine's Catholic Primary School, Old Costessey

Eggs' Story

Once upon a time, there lived a teddy bear called Eggs. He was purple, yellow, pink and blue. One day, we were sorting boxes before moving for 'charity', 'dump' and 'loft'. I put him the loft pile but he jumped into the charity box because he thought we had put him in the dump pile.

When we moved house we could not find him and I was very sad about that. I will always wonder what Eggs' new family are like. I hope they will love him as much as I loved my teddy. Hopefully he might come back soon.

Elizabeth Anne Mitchell (7)

St Augustine's Catholic Primary School, Old Costessey

Those Naughty Toys!

Once, there lived a little girl and her name was Daisy. Sometimes she wonders what naughty things they might get up to. By 'they' I mean her toys in her toy box. Daisy was already late for school and wished she had taken her skates out. Whilst Daisy was at school, her rag doll had taken the skates into the kitchen. You should have seen the mess! After that, all of the toys came out and caused havoc! Mr Ted had eaten all the biscuits and left loads of crumbs. When Daisy got there she cried, "What, help!"

Ava Antonia Baxter (7)
St Augustine's Catholic Primary School, Old Costessey

The Unicorn Night Adventure

One night I went to sleep, then the adventure started. When I was sleeping, all of my fluffy toys came alive. First of all, they had hot chocolate. Then after, they had it they came upstairs. They played a bit and then they had a disco. It was quite long. At the disco they played games and were silly, they really enjoyed that.
That's when I woke up. The toys didn't have time to escape so they froze. I went back to sleep. That's when they went back to their places because it was getting early.

Gabi Maria Moszczenska (8)
St Augustine's Catholic Primary School, Old Costessey

The Fun Day

Once upon a time, a cat called Mable and a dog called Caremel woke up. They went to the park and played on the monkey bars. A few minutes later, their friends came to join them. It was Thunder the horse and Pecky the parrot. They tried playing 'fly behind' but the only one who could fly was Pecky. Thunder said, "Why don't we play races as we can all run and Pecky could fly?" They thought it was a good idea but they had to go. When they got home, they went back where they were. They'd had fun.

Emilia Sojka (7)
St Augustine's Catholic Primary School, Old Costessey

Dominoes

Once upon a time, there was a little boy called Tom who liked playing with dominoes. Every morning, all of his dominoes were set up by themselves and he couldn't figure out why. He decided to stay up but that did not work because he got so tired and fell asleep again. The second night he stayed awake, but he did not see anything and was very disappointed, so on the third night he set up a video and guess what he saw? The glittering tooth fairy was setting up the dominoes with her magic. The strange mystery was solved!

Darci-Ella Knott (7)
St Augustine's Catholic Primary School, Old Costessey

Mya's Exciting Adventure To Toys 'R' Us

Mya was in Argos. There was no one to play with. She was so bored. No one wanted to buy her. She heard stories of a place called Toys 'R' Us. She wanted to go there. Then she escaped. She ran down the street, round the corner and down the alley. There was Toys 'R' Us. She went inside, it was full of toys, lots of toys. She saw Lalaloopsy, Baby Alives and teddies. She ran down the aisle. She went to the dolls. Then she saw her friends. She stayed a long, long time and made lots of friends.

Pemisin Akinsiku (7)
St Augustine's Catholic Primary School, Old Costessey

Santa Woody Is Coming To Town

It's nearly Christmas time so Woody decided to be Santa Claus. He saw a Christmas costume shop and asked the shop helper if they had a Santa suit. When she came back, she gave him a Mrs Santa costume.

Woody said, "But I am a boy."

"Sorry but that is the last one," she said.

Then Woody had a deep thought, *I will call Jessie.* In the end, Jessie came as Mrs Santa and Woody came as an elf. It doesn't matter who you are, what matters is giving and sharing.

Andre Dimaandal (7)
St Augustine's Catholic Primary School, Old Costessey

Boot Choccy-Woccy Paw Prints

I kissed Bobo goodbye as I left for school. When Bobo heard the door shut, he sneaked downstairs to visit Boot. Bobo's tummy was rumbling like thunder. He crept into the kitchen and Boot helped Bobo into the cupboard to get a delicious cake. Bobo ate the cake, leaving a chocolatey mess with paw prints everywhere. Then she heard a key in the door, locked Boot in his cage, joined the other toys on the bed and went still. When we came home, we saw chocolate prints everywhere and poor Boot got blamed.

Angela Gabriella Thomas (7)

St Augustine's Catholic Primary School, Old Costessey

The Secret Slumber Party

Once upon a time, there was a family of Beanie Boos that belonged to a girl called Kate. The toys decided to be really sneaky and have a slumber party. They crawled off the bed and the leader, Wishful the unicorn, guided them to her closet. A few hours later, Kate came in and got dressed to go to the shop. The Beanie Boos tried to get out but there was no way out. The leader shouted, "Shh, we need to look like clothes!" But Kate came in and put them in time out. "No!"

Kate Garchitorena (8)
St Augustine's Catholic Primary School, Old Costessey

The Nasty Eagle

When I was in bed, a toy owl looked out the window. It was a baby owl. The owl was looking out for other owls to play with. He saw something and thought it was an owl, but when he got closer he saw it was an eagle! He was nice at first, for a long time. Then he set traps for baby owls. The eagle was about to eat him when suddenly, another owl swooped down to annoy the eagle so the baby owl could escape. He went back home and said, "Maybe it's safer to stay at home."

Ben Schiller (7)

St Augustine's Catholic Primary School, Old Costessey

The Great Adventure

One day, the toys were bored so they planned what they were going to do. As soon as they finished, they set off. First they found the toy box, they all climbed up so they jumped in. After they finished playing in it, they all climbed out. When they climbed out, they found the giant unicorn toy. The unicorn toy said, "Climb on my back," and they all did.

Five minutes later, the girl came. All the toys ran in their positions.

Jhenzel Daleon (8)
St Augustine's Catholic Primary School, Old Costessey

Friendship

Woody and his friend, Bullseye, went to visit a castle. Woody got into the castle and Bullseye waited outside. Woody got trapped inside and he cried loudly. Bullseye heard his cry and he tried to go inside the castle, but the security would not allow him to go inside. So he ran to Woody's girlfriend's house and told her about the trap. She came to the castle and saved Woody from the trap, and the three of them returned home happy.

Andre Alphons (8)

St Augustine's Catholic Primary School, Old Costessey

The Last Nazi

Once upon a time, there was a Lego soldier called Noodle. He had built himself a house out of Lego. The toy soldiers warned Noodle that the last Nazi was coming to get him and he had a machine gun. Noodle hurried outside to face him. He jumped but it was too late! The Nazi grabbed him and put him in prison in a balloon world.

Howard James Burke (7)
St Augustine's Catholic Primary School, Old Costessey

Run For It!

We ran away from that horrible Rubber Man, he was trying to erase us. He always does that but we always get away from him.

"Scram! Split!" Sergeant screamed.

We darted our own ways, Harry and I hid under the cupboard as still as mice, but Rubber Man spotted us. "We're doomed!"

The battle had begun, Rubber Man vs Toys, we couldn't decide on a name.

"Incoming!" Sergeant Whisper shouted.

"Yes!" Sergeant was with us. We buried ourselves deeper into the cupboard, worrying. Rubber Man spotted us.

"Yikes!" said Tom. "He's looking at us."

"Run for it!" Sergeant Whisper shouted.

Olivia Marie Archer (9)

St Mary's Roman Catholic Primary School, Lowestoft

Lego Criminal Forge

"We're here, troops," said Sicore. "Let's fight!"
The Lego criminals started in New York and
absolutely dismantled Algeria, and were about to
start in London when they were busted by riot
police. The criminals called for backup and their
land ship called Earthbreaker. The criminal general
was called Thorpe. Sicore, the leader, and the team
started battling. The riot police called for backup
too. They rode in their jeeps and cornered the
criminals and stunned them before sending them
to prison. A few weeks later, the criminals found a
way to escape and began planning their next
attack...

Samuel Amias Buhr (8)
St Mary's Roman Catholic Primary School, Lowestoft

Techno Warriors In Winter

The evil Nemus had made a weather machine to make everyone really cold, hot or wet. He used the snow to make all the Techno Warriors freeze. Except Captain Thermo who used his heat protection to block the ice. Nemus took all the Techno Warriors' pets with special powers and turned them into ordinary people. Captain Thermo called on Mirror Man who lived in Portugal. Mirror Man was able to deflect the ice and snow as they fought with the evil Nemus. They saved the other Techno Warriors but their pets were still ordinary. Don't forget, Techno Warriors always win.

Thomas Sewell (7)
St Mary's Roman Catholic Primary School, Lowestoft

Miss Prissy

The day had gone, I brushed my teeth, got into my comfy bed and fell asleep. Then I heard horses' hooves trotting in the distance. I woke up as I heard noises. Then I noticed Miss Prissy and Charlotte were missing.

"Where are they? What will I tell my mum?"

I went downstairs, my mum said, "We'll look for them in the morning."

Overnight, Miss Prissy and Charlotte had the time of their lives riding. Eventually, they came home to the places they were left.

When I woke up, they were exactly where I left them.

Naomi Eleanor Sibbons (9)

St Mary's Roman Catholic Primary School, Lowestoft

Midnight Feast Party

It's a cold, dark night and Ella the toy goblin was getting ready to party with Brooke, Polly, Ronan and Kian. At the party the disco started.
"Whoop, whoop, Gangnam Style! I love this song!" shouted Ella Goblin. Ella the goblin loves to dance, her dancing was that crazy she went back and, *smash!* The music stopped. The speaker fell over, everyone laughed and it made her sad!
Brooke went over and gave her a hug. "Don't worry, it's now the midnight feast, I've saved you some of your favourite cake!"

Brooke LJ Matthews (8)

St Mary's Roman Catholic Primary School, Lowestoft

The Stolen Unicorn

In London, a girl called India loved toys, especially unicorns. She heard about a new toyshop. She emptied out her money box but she only had two pence. India skipped down the road to the toyshop anyway, she looked inside but there was no magical unicorn there. She sighed, "No fun for me!" She had an idea. India crept along to the 'Staff Only' door and pushed it open. "Ooooh," she said. Standing in front of her was a rainbow unicorn. All her dreams and wishes had come true. India stuffed it into her pocket and ran off.

Thea Jackson-Tennant (9)

St Mary's Roman Catholic Primary School, Lowestoft

The Short Robot On A Shelf

Once upon a time, there lived a lonely robot on a shelf in a stock room. He was different from all the others, he was small and squeaky, the others laughed and made fun of him, called him Squeaky and left him out.

Day by day he watched the other robots being picked up by happy, smiling children and taken to loving homes. Squeaky thought he'd never be chosen. Roby had exactly the same problem. She was small and always left out. They were a perfect match.

She bought Squeaky and took him to a loving home. He loved it.

Mya Mckenna Reay-Smith (8)
St Mary's Roman Catholic Primary School, Lowestoft

The Mischievous Toys

One summer's morning, a girl named Amelia decided to go for a walk in the woods. On her walk she saw lots of amazing creatures.

Meanwhile, all of her toys were coming alive and destroying everything. First, they all rushed over to Amelia's white pristine cupboard and frantically started flinging clothes across the room like they were crazy. Then they marched downstairs and started smashing nicely patterned plates and bowls. When Amelia got home, she was sent to her room and wasn't allowed any electronics for a week.

Chaeli Knights (10)
St Mary's Roman Catholic Primary School, Lowestoft

The Cuddly Cat

In 1966, a cuddly cat called Molly lived in a castle with a little princess. While the princess was out, Molly climbed up the turrets to get the best view. She saw a door made out of red leaves big enough to fit through. It led to a mouse kingdom where she was surrounded by mice. Excitedly, she caught all the scared, grey finger puppet mice, except four. These quick, clever mice hid in the forest, until Molly left. They came out of hiding and had the kingdom all to themselves, where they lived happily. Molly went home full up!

Holly Burrows (7)

St Mary's Roman Catholic Primary School, Lowestoft

Lucas' Christmas Elf

One morning, not just any morning, it was Christmas for a very special little girl called Lucy. She was very excited because she asked for an elf and she was hoping. Then she saw the tree with lots of presents. The first one she saw she picked up and it was the elf, so she opened the rest of the presents then went to get dressed. The elf came with a collection so they came alive and turned to a workshop and started making things out of Christmas tree decorations and who knows what might happen next?

Gabrielle Elizabeth Lock (10)
St Mary's Roman Catholic Primary School, Lowestoft

Toy Soldiers

It was a cold, misty night when it all began. The toy soldiers marched into battle. The small toys marched up the stairs. All of a sudden, they were sucked into a video game. They marched all day and all night, over boiling-hot land and freezing-cold land. They fought hundreds of wars, losing loads of men until there was only one fierce soldier left. All of a sudden, it was morning and he was no longer in the video game.

A nine-year-old boy wondered where his soldiers were.

Elijah Huke-Jenner (9)

St Mary's Roman Catholic Primary School, Lowestoft

Untitled

Once, I went to a toyshop. I saw this amazing toy and its name was Dooby, and it could do anything but not turn alive. Suddenly, there were three more toys called Zoe, Spat and Munchkin and I found out that Zoe could come alive.

Eventually, Zoe arrived in London and got into a fight with Thomas and they kept punching each other. I called the police and quickly hid Zoe so that she didn't get told off.

Kailan Ansley (9)
St Mary's Roman Catholic Primary School, Lowestoft

The Mystery

Sally just left home. Suddenly, the ponies started talking.

"There is a mystery that needs to be solved," whispered Flapjack.

"We must solve it!" chanted the rest of the herd, as they crept out to start searching.

They crept along the deserted corridor until they found a trapdoor. However, when they all crept in they saw the front of a box.

"What's in there?" they whispered.

When they opened it, they found a rare pony.

When Sally finally arrived home, she saw the pony. In the living room she found all the ponies scattered on the carpet.

"What?" Sally exclaimed.

Isobel Bond (8)
Tattingstone CE (VC) Primary School, Tattingstone

A Weird But Wonderful Day

I awoke remembering that I got left in Toys 'R' Us whilst Christmas shopping with my family. It had been torture because there were so many great toys I'd wanted. I couldn't believe it; suddenly, all around me were toys coming to life! Skateboards whizzing past, balls bouncing, Lego figures playing, Nerfs firing and toy planes flying above. I leapt up onto a hoverboard and zoomed around the aisles, dodging RC car wheels spinning on the tiles. For hours I played with the amazing toys, until eventually I sat exhaustedly and wondered if my family were wondering where I was...

George Seager (10)
Tattingstone CE (VC) Primary School, Tattingstone

Untitled

"Twenty-nine, thirty, ready or not here I come! Hmm, where could they be?"

"I've got a great idea, he'll never find us here."

"What! In the box of giant teddies? That's the dumbest idea you've had yet! I'm going to hide behind the gigantic Geoffrey the giraffe, he'll never find me there."

Then, from the window of the wooden playhouse, Adam noticed that the store was not as busy as when he'd started to count. Suddenly, it went dark! The only sound that could be heard was the clink of the keys as they turned in the door...

Layton Palmer (10)
Tattingstone CE (VC) Primary School, Tattingstone

The Old Attic Bear

Once, there was an old attic bear who had been long forgotten, so one day in the dead of night, the attic bear, aka Joey, came to life! He decided to climb out of the attic and down into his master's bedroom. He climbed through the hall, the kitchen and the sitting room and finally came to the bedroom.

"Phew!" Joey said.

They climbed into the cosy toy box.

"Who are you?" the toys asked.

"I'm Joey."

"Come in," said everyone.

Later, everybody was tired, so they all went to sleep together in the toy box, including Joey the Bear.

Mia Joseph (9)
Tattingstone CE (VC) Primary School, Tattingstone

Magic Fairy In Toys 'R' Us

"Quick, quick, we must hide behind the well and make sure she doesn't see us!" Holly was worried as she didn't want the giant human to take her out of her garden. "Oh look, she's watering the grass seed but we need to sprinkle the fairy dust everywhere otherwise it won't grow!"
The grass and flowers started to shoot and the little mouse looked over at 'Cloud' the unicorn. "Arr! Wow! The fairy garden has come to life. This means there will be a rainbow." Holly climbed onto Cloud and trotted over to see the start of the rainbow magic.

Holly Abbott (9)
Tattingstone CE (VC) Primary School, Tattingstone

Ginger's Unheard Adventures

One cold, damp night, I decided to go for a walk. Suddenly, I heard a loud noise. I did not know what it was, so I hid in a cave.

"There's a storm coming," said a ghostly voice.

I stayed in the cave for a couple of hours until it stopped.

"Breakfast is ready, Bob."

My nose began to twitch. I could smell some cucumber. "Mmm, my favourite!" There was a bright light. I opened my eyes slowly. I'd been in a dream.

I was in Bob's room all along, together with the other toys on Bob's comfy, warm bed.

Samuel Cocksedge (9)
Tattingstone CE (VC) Primary School, Tattingstone

Midnight Chime

One Christmas Eve, in the Toys 'R' Us store, was a girl called Lily who went through a special Lego door. On the other side, in the corner, a magical unicorn sat, followed by a fluffy, ginger cat. The unicorn, Sparkles, took Lily on an adventure she'd never forget.

In and out through the different aisles, Sparkles shouted, "These shelves stacked with toys go on for miles!"

The two of them played for hours, stacking the toys into tall, steep towers. Sadly Lily had to go, it was past her bedtime, she had to be asleep before the midnight chime...

Lily Mae Ransome (11)

Tattingstone CE (VC) Primary School, Tattingstone

Toys 'R' Us Help Santa

One day, Truffles and Flamingo were helping the other toys get the shop ready for Christmas and Santa coming too! That very next day it was Christmas Eve and then Santa would be coming to collect them.

It was Christmas Eve, already they were waiting for Santa to come and collect them. Suddenly, they heard a crash and some of them rushed out of the shop. Santa had broken his sleigh, and so the toys helped him fix his sleigh and deliver themselves happily to the good sleeping children before sunrise. When the children woke up, they were happy.

Francesca Goodwin (9)
Tattingstone CE (VC) Primary School, Tattingstone

The Forgotten Wood

Fin is a toy fox, a playful chap. But one day a badger came by and said, "What's your name? My name is Badgy." Fin was scared, it was night-time so Badgy said, "I will help you."
They entered the deep, dark wood. They talked and they laughed but then they heard a bang! Fin got scared, so he dug a hole for himself and then a mystical frog came and they partied till dawn. Now Fin wasn't scared, he was happy and he lived happily ever after. They were the most happy family in the deep, dark wood ever!

Alana Goodwin (8)
Tattingstone CE (VC) Primary School, Tattingstone

The Shop Around The Corner

There once was a little girl, Ruby, she was homeless and dreamed of being a ballerina. She lived in a doorway with her mum and dad. There was a toyshop around the corner and in the window stood a beautiful ballerina. Ruby wanted it so much but she couldn't afford it. A lady gave her five shiny pound coins, the ballerina cost £4.50. Ruby was hungry so she gave the money to her parents for food. Her parents already had food, so they bought the ballerina. Ruby woke on Christmas Day and saw her beautiful ballerina, she was overjoyed.

Isabel Knights (10)
Tattingstone CE (VC) Primary School, Tattingstone

Tinsel Snake's Adventure

A Tinsel Snake who had no friends slithered into Toys 'R' Us and he met a Fingerling and they became friends. The Fingerling showed Tinsel Snake around the shop. Tinsel Snake said it was extraordinary and wanted to stay forever. They played hide-and-seek and board games and wrote their letters for Santa. Tinsel Snake had never been so happy. He never wanted to leave. They decided to stay together and hide when it was morning so no one bought them! Every night they came out and played new games and also went on new exciting adventures.

Olive Potter-Cobbold (9)
Tattingstone CE (VC) Primary School, Tattingstone

The Toyshop Catastrophe

Once there was a toyshop, quiet and still. At night the toys in the toyshop came alive. Tonight was a special night, Mr Piggy Winkles was going to space! But first he had to build his rocket.
"This will be fun!" he said and hopped right to it. He had nearly finished when King Doff, Mr Piggy Winkles' sheep nemesis, stole the engine for the rocket. Mr Piggy Winkles ran after him and took it back. He ran back, quickly put it in the rocket and jumped in. He took one last look at the toyshop. Soon he was off!

Molly Wheatley (11)
Tattingstone CE (VC) Primary School, Tattingstone

Unicorn Holiday

Once upon a time, a little girl had a unicorn named Paris Glitter Sparkle. She loved the unicorn so much. A week later she went on a holiday to Paris for a week. She was at the airport waiting for her plane to come around the corner and it came two minutes later.

She said, "When will we be there?"

Then they went through customs to get on the plane and she went to Paris. Her unicorn got lost. They looked everywhere. Then her dad found the unicorn in her bag. They lived happily ever after and always loved unicorns.

Lilly Mai King (10)
Tattingstone CE (VC) Primary School, Tattingstone

Magic In The Toyshop

Ever wondered why you pick the toy you buy? There is a rumour that years ago a shiny metal toy truck fell off a shelf onto the floor. Over time he became dull and dusty, but every single day, year after year he helped all the other toys find their new homes by making sure they were on the shelf and looking their best. One day he felt a hand pick him up, it was the store manager. "I have been looking for one of these for ages."

He took him home and shone him up. He called him Sorusty.

Corban Zak Louka (9)

Tattingstone CE (VC) Primary School, Tattingstone

The Bedtime Uprising

"Get to bed now, boy!" echoed a hollow voice from the small ladder leading to a dark, worn corridor. "OK," stuttered the young boy. With no hesitation, Hank rushed to his bed, in fear of getting locked up in the cellar for the night.

You see, having left their home, the poor boy was never loved by his parents.

Little does Hank know, that in the night his dreams become reality, as his repeated wish is granted. Every night, as the moon comes into view, a toy from Hank's dream roams the streets, in search of the next dreamer.

Isabella Hackett Morillo (11)
Walpole Cross Keys Primary School, King's Lynn

The Naughty Fish

"Hello, I'm Goldie, the fish."
"Wow, it's raining!" confessed Goldie the toy fish. "I should go outside!"
So she did but it started to snow, she could not bear it so she came inside but then the door opened. An ominous figure stood there waving in the snow then the ominous figure came in. Later on, she sat down for tea then she said, "Is it bedtime yet?"
The mum said, "Of course it's not, why would you even think that?"
"Now it's night-time, silly."
"Goodnight, Mum."
"Goodnight, darling."
"Love you."
"See you later, Mum."
"Bye."

Milly Nudds (7)
Wells-Next-The-Sea Primary And Nursery, Wells-Next-The-Sea

What Bunny Gets Up To

"Now what should I do today?" muttered Bunny. *Hmm!* Bunny thought for a while. "I will hide Lily's clothes," yelled Bunny. "Ha, ha, ha!" screamed Bunny. "I will put them in the dollhouse, she will never find them there!" squealed Bunny.

Just then, as the door creaked open, a flash of light flashed in Lily's eyes. "Argh! I can't see!" shrieked Lily. "Let's play dolls, why are there clothes in my doll's house?" complained Lily. "And why are you over there?" asked Lily. "It must be Jessica." Lily gasped. "I knew it! Jessica!"

Lily Wines (7)

Wells-Next-The-Sea Primary And Nursery, Wells-Next-The-Sea

The Doll That Messed Up The Bedroom

"Oh, what's in here?" whispered the doll, Lauren. Lauren looked amazed at how many clothes Frances had, so she started to pull them out. *Pull! Pull! Pull!* "Uh-oh!" After five seconds, they were all out of her wardrobe. Then, Lauren waddled over to the chest of drawers and did the same thing there. She made lots of mess.

Suddenly, the door creaked open and in came Frances. Frances couldn't believe how much mess there was.

Frances shouted, "Issy, how dare you?"

From the corner Frances heard an extremely quiet giggle. She turned. "What was that noise? I must be dreaming."

Frances Emmerton (7)

Wells-Next-The-Sea Primary And Nursery, Wells-Next-The-Sea

The Fate Of The Toys

When I left my bedroom, I put Baloo on my bed.
Baloo wondered how many toys I had.
He said, "Wow!" He pulled my toys out bit by bit,
he said, "Go, go, go, come on, pull the toys out!"
All of my other toys said, "What?"
"Come on!"
"No!"
"Yes, do what I say!"
"No! No! No!"
"Hollie's coming, prepare to fight."
He froze like normal. When I came in I shouted,
"Seth! Seth! Seth!"
He cried. I picked up Baloo safely. I snuggled down
with him and watched the sun set as we fell asleep
on the grass.

Hollie Ellen Lovick (7)
Wells-Next-The-Sea Primary And Nursery, Wells-Next-The-
Sea

What Milla Gets Up To

"Can I be mischievous?" whispered Milla. So Milla went to Evie's toy cupboard. One minute later, Milla got all the toys out of the cupboard and played with all her toys. First, she played tick tock clock, then went outside and played on the swings. Finally, small Milla went back inside. Then she heard a creak on the door.

"Evie's back, hide!" shouted Milla.

Evie gently picked up Milla and put her back on her bed.

Evie shouted, "Oscar! Oscar, why did you go in my room? Go into your bedroom now Oscar, or I'll tell you off!"

Evie Moore (7)
Wells-Next-The-Sea Primary And Nursery, Wells-Next-The-Sea

In The Kitchen

In Alfie's new bedroom, the Xbox crept off charge when Alfie wasn't looking. "Good he's still asleep," Xbox 360 whispered to himself. He crept downstairs to the kitchen and gobbled up the cereal and drank all the milk. "That's not bad."
As soon as it was morning, Alfie woke up and when he saw his Xbox was gone he said, "How did my Xbox get away?"
He went downstairs to search for his Xbox and found it in the kitchen. Alfie took his Xbox back upstairs but forgot to put it back! Alfie went downstairs. The Xbox was a disaster.

Alfie Yaxley-Beckham (8)

Wells-Next-The-Sea Primary And Nursery, Wells-Next-The-Sea

Thinker

One grey day, I was sleeping in my cosy, warm bed, not knowing that my toy came to life. He fearlessly jumped out my window into the hedge. He raced all round the forest and around my lovely house. I woke up and wondered where my toy was.

Later on, my Slinky was on a search for him. "Argh!" moaned Slinky, "I never thought this would happen," squeaked Slinky. "Well, off I go!" He set off on a big journey to find the toy.

Finding my toy after hours, I whispered, "Come on, we've got to go home. Let's walk."

Toby Wright (7)
Wells-Next-The-Sea Primary And Nursery, Wells-Next-The-Sea

Robot In Trouble

I left my big blue bedroom. I screamed, "Bye-bye!" to my big epic robot.

Suddenly he screamed, "It is clear, I am going to destroy the bedroom!" so he did. He destroyed my Lego, my bed. Next he saw it all, he whispered, "What have I done?"

Robot realised he was going to get told off. He was scared.

A few minutes later, he found his friends and played with them. They had so much fun until the human came and shouted, "What!" and then he built the Lego again and it was all together.

Zachary Long (7)
Wells-Next-The-Sea Primary And Nursery, Wells-Next-The-Sea

Take Down

"Come on, roll in quickly," shouted Blue Eyes.

"Go, go, go!" screamed Uncal.

So we went upstairs and tidied the room. A boy came in. All slinkies froze. Then our owner noticed us and put us away. Then we jumped out and hid. The door opened, no one was there, it was creepy so we left and went downstairs and then the owner came back from the shop.

"Go on Sam," cried Blue Eyes, and they took the owner down and got a victory now again.

"Yes, yes, yes!" screamed Bluey.

George Wright (8)
Wells-Next-The-Sea Primary And Nursery, Wells-Next-The-Sea

Untitled

When Tedster was alone and no one was there, Tedster wrecked my room until everything was everywhere. Soon I was back and my room was wrecked! Meanwhile, "I am back!" I shouted. "Someone wrecked my room!"

My mum told me to tidy my room. When I tidied my room, it was messed up again. My mum thought I'd messed it up again and looked around me and my room was tidy! In the end, I did the same thing every time so my naughty teddy would never do it ever again.

Robert Smith (7)

Wells-Next-The-Sea Primary And Nursery, Wells-Next-The-Sea

The Bad Bear

"Yes, yes, yes, my owner is gone, now I can mess the room up, pull the sign down, kill the other toys," cried Charlie, the bear.
Then I yelled, "What are you doing you naughty, silly, soft Charlie the bear?"
Then Charlie the bear was nice and safe in my cosy, warm, cool bed.
But the next morning, he ran downstairs and ripped all of my presents open. But he did not open all of my presents, so when we went out for tea we left Charlie the naughty bear at home.

Lily-Grace Jones (7)
Wells-Next-The-Sea Primary And Nursery, Wells-Next-The-Sea

Silly Slinkies!

One day when I wasn't at my house, all my slinkies trashed my room. They smashed my window, broke my bed and everything. I did not know what to do. I screamed. I thought it was my little brother but then I thought again. I was like, no, it couldn't be him, it must be my slinkies; they all like to prank me all the time. I must get them back but I don't know what to tell them. I will just tell them to not do it again. No, I will tell them to tidy the house.

Marley Daniels (8)
Wells-Next-The-Sea Primary And Nursery, Wells-Next-The-Sea

The Naughty Bear

When I left the house for school, my teddy jumped off my bed and trashed my room and next she trashed the living room. At 2 o'clock, she had a nap. At 3 o'clock, she woke up and watched TV in the living room and ten hours later, I got home from school. I went to do my homework. The next day, I went to school. My teddy tidied my room, it was a mission. I was grounded for ten weeks because my room was a massive mess, so I cleaned my room and the next week it was clean.

Ann-Marie Needham (7)
Wells-Next-The-Sea Primary And Nursery, Wells-Next-The-Sea

Untitled

Once upon a time, the crane moved when I was not there. The crane was on my bed and he knocked down the bar, and he went down the stairs and blamed it on my baby brother. He went down the stairs and went outside and wrecked the path. He went on the road and he dug a hole. He went to the shop and smashed the window, went up the stairs in the shop and smashed the escalators. He went back home and went outside, and smashed my go-kart and I got angry. He sat down.

Cody-Liam Wyatt Lacey (7)
Wells-Next-The-Sea Primary And Nursery, Wells-Next-The-Sea

Trash Time

Batman was playing with Joker. Then he lost him. Then Batman was looking for Joker and when he found him he shouted, "Do you want to trash their room?"
Joker said, "Yes!" and when it was trashed they had a fight over a toy, but Batman won so Joker got in a tank and went home.
I saw Joker in a tank aiming at Batman. I tidied up my room. The next day, I saw it was trashed again and I always have to tidy it up.

Freddie William Bix (7)
Wells-Next-The-Sea Primary And Nursery, Wells-Next-The-Sea

 Young**Writers**

Est.1991

YOUNG WRITERS
INFORMATION

We hope you have enjoyed reading this book – and that you will continue to in the coming years.

If you're a young writer who enjoys reading and creative writing, or the parent of an enthusiastic poet or story writer, do visit our website **www.youngwriters.co.uk**. Here you will find free competitions, workshops and games, as well as recommended reads, a poetry glossary and our blog.

If you would like to order further copies of this book, or any of our other titles, then please give us a call or visit **www.youngwriters.co.uk**.

Young Writers
Remus House
Coltsfoot Drive
Peterborough
PE2 9BF
(01733) 890066 / 898110
info@youngwriters.co.uk

 @YoungWritersUK    @YoungWritersCW